# Asha
## and the
## Toymaker

Sakshi Mangal

Kids Can Press

I live with my papa and my dog, Moti.

Papa makes the best wooden toys in India.

He spends every day from morning till evening selling his toys at the market. He does this so he can send me to school.

Papa tries very hard to find customers
by showing his handcrafted wooden toys
to everyone who passes by.

Some days, Papa comes home without selling any toys at all.
I know that he worries.
I also know that sometimes Papa goes to bed hungry because he has only enough money to buy food for me.

While my papa is out, I spend my time after school painting everything I can find. A little bit of colorful paint makes anything beautiful.

I paint kites,

my study chair,

the inside of the cupboard

and even Moti!

One night, while I'm busy painting in my bedroom, I get an idea.

"Papa! Papa! I know how you can sell more toys. All you need is some color. I can paint them bright!"

But Papa doesn't like my idea.

"That's not your job, Asha," he says. "Your job is to study hard and go to school. Now go and finish your homework."

But I want to help my papa sell
his toys.
Instead of doing my homework,
I sneak downstairs to his workshop.

One by one, I paint his toys all the colors of the rainbow. They are more beautiful than all the other toys in the marketplace.

In the morning, Papa is upset.
"Asha," he says, "I told you to finish your homework."
"But Papa," I say, "I want to help you."

Papa doesn't listen. "I have to sell toys because I was not able to study as a child. I don't want you to waste your time painting. I want you to study hard so you can get a good job one day. Then you will never have to go to bed hungry."

As Papa leaves, he sounds disappointed. "All that time wasted."

Through the small window, I see Papa looking more worried than ever. But then I hear a shout. Children surround him.

There are so many children!
I see a little boy rocking on a lakdi ki kathi.
I see a little girl twirling a colorful damaru.

I come out of the house to get a closer look. Papa smiles at me from above the crowd—a smile as bright as a rainbow. I run straight into Papa's arms.

"Asha," he says, "you were right!"

The next day, Papa gives me a big box of new paints.

"Will you paint all my toys from now on?" he asks.

I hug my papa tight.

"Yes, Papa! Of course I will!"

Now I paint all the toys my papa makes.
And sometimes, as long as my homework
is done, I join Papa at the market.

**Papa, thanks for always believing in me. This one's for you. — S.M.**

## Author's Note

Growing up in Mumbai, India, I loved to paint, and I loved going to the market with my family. The street vendors were fascinating to me, especially the ones who sold colorful toys. I would spend hours looking at the way the toys were cleverly stacked together on wooden stands.

In the story, Asha's papa hadn't been able to study as a child because his family was poor. At a very young age, he would have had to take up the responsibility of helping his father earn money to feed his family. He would have spent his childhood working to earn money instead of studying. That's why it's so important to him that Asha has time to study and dream about a better future.

Unlike Asha, I did not have to convince my father to let me paint. For me, believing in myself was the real challenge. I hope Asha is an inspiration to all of you to pursue your dreams, no matter how difficult. Anything is possible if you believe you can do it, just like Asha believed she could help her papa.

Published in Canada and the U.S. by Kids Can Press Ltd.
25 Dockside Drive, Toronto, ON  M5A 0B5

Kids Can Press is a Corus Entertainment Inc. company

www.kidscanpress.com

The artwork in this book was rendered using a combination of colored pencils, block prints, acrylic paints and brush pens and finished digitally.

The text is set in Albert Sans.

Edited by Patricia Ocampo
Designed by Marie Bartholomew

Printed and bound in Shenzhen, China, in 3/2023
by C & C Offset

FSC
www.fsc.org
MIX
Paper | Supporting
responsible forestry
FSC® C008047

CM 23  0 9 8 7 6 5 4 3 2 1

**Library and Archives Canada Cataloguing in Publication**
Title: Asha and the toymaker / Sakshi Mangal.
Names: Mangal, Sakshi, author, illustrator.
Identifiers: Canadiana (print) 20220460434 | Canadiana (ebook) 20220460442 | ISBN 9781525306662 (hardcover) | ISBN 9781525308161 (EPUB)
Subjects: LCGFT: Picture books. | LCGFT: Fiction.
Classification: LCC PS8626.A556 A91 2023 | DDC jC813/.6 — dc23

Kids Can Press gratefully acknowledges that the land on which our office is located is the traditional territory of many nations, including the Mississaugas of the Credit, the Anishnabeg, the Chippewa, the Haudenosaunee and the Wendat peoples, and is now home to many diverse First Nations, Inuit and Métis peoples.

We thank the Government of Ontario, through Ontario Creates, for supporting our publishing activity.